Random House / Children's Television Workshop

Library of Congress Cataloging in Publication Data:
Elliott, Dan. My doll is lost. (A Sesame Street start-to-read book) SUMMARY: When he and his doll are invited to Bert and Ernie's party, Herry Monster discovers his doll is missing. [1. Dolls–Fiction. 2. Lost and found possessions–Fiction. 3. Puppets–Fiction] I. Mathieu, Joseph, ill. II. Title. III. Series: Sesame Street start-to-read books. PZ7.E446My 1984 [E] 83-11211 ISBN: 0-394-86251-1 (trade); 0-394-96251-6 (lib. bdg.) Manufactured in the United States of America   4 5 6 7 8 9 0

A Sesame Street Start-to-Read Book™

My Doll Is Lost!

by Dan Elliott • illustrated by Joe Mathieu

Featuring Jim Henson's Sesame Street Muppets

U.S. POST OFFICE

Herry Monster liked to skip.
One day he skipped
down Sesame Street...
and right into the mailman.
Letters went flying.
So did the mailman.

Herry helped the mailman get up.

Then he picked up the letters.

"Look!" said Herry.

"A letter for ME!"

Herry dropped his bag

and read the letter.

The letter said:

"Come to a tea party today.

Bring your favorite doll."

It was from Ernie and Bert.

Herry skipped down the block.
"I love parties!" he sang.
He skipped to Betty Lou's house.
She had a letter too.

"Are you going to the party?"
he asked her.
"Oh, yes," she said.
"And so is my beautiful doll."
Herry smiled and said,
"So is MY beautiful doll."
Then Herry stopped smiling.
"Where IS my doll?"

Suddenly Herry remembered.
"I had my doll in a bag
and I put it down on a pile
of leaves by the post office."
Betty Lou said, "Let's go find it."

They ran to the post office.
But the pile of leaves was gone.
"Someone raked up the leaves,"
said Betty Lou.
"And my doll too!" cried Herry.

"Don't cry," said Betty Lou.
"I will help you find your doll.
 What does it look like?"
 Herry thought about his doll.
"Oh, he is the most beautiful doll
 in the world," he said.

"Then it must look like my doll!" said Betty Lou. And she ran off to look for a beautiful doll.

Just then Grover came along.

"My doll is lost!" yelled Herry.

"What does your doll look like?"
asked Grover.

Herry thought about his doll.

"He is soft and fuzzy," said Herry.

"My doll is soft and fuzzy too.
Do not be sad.
I, Grover the Finder,
will find your doll."
And Grover ran off.

Herry walked by the bakery.

Cookie Monster waved to him.

"Herry!" yelled Cookie.

"Why you look sad?"

"My doll is lost," said Herry.

"And he is so sweet!"

Cookie shook his head sadly.

"My doll sweet too!"

Then he gave Herry a cookie.

"Cookie make you happy," he said.

Herry nibbled at the cookie.
He was so sad he did not watch
where he was walking.
He walked right into Big Bird.

"Herry!" said Big Bird.

"What's the matter?"

Herry told Big Bird about his doll.

"And I cannot go to the party

without my doll," cried Herry.

"Poor Herry!" said Big Bird.

"What does your doll look like?"

Herry thought about his doll.

"He is cuddly.

And he is very nice."

"Gee," said Big Bird,
"your doll sounds just like mine.
I will look for it.
It will be easy to find."
And Big Bird ran off.

Herry sat down by a trash can.
"It is nice to have friends
who want to help.
But I still feel AWFUL!"
he said to himself.

"WHERE IS MY DOLL?"
he yelled out loud.
Up popped Oscar the Grouch.
"NO YELLING ALLOWED!"
yelled Oscar.

Herry began to cry again.
"I think my doll was thrown away
with the trash," he cried.
Oscar's eyes lit up.
"What does your doll look like?"

"He is beautiful," Herry said.

"Hmmm," said Oscar.

"I found a beautiful doll
in the trash this morning."
And he went down into his can.

Soon Oscar popped up again.
He had a doll with a torn dress
and one arm gone.
"Is this your doll?" asked Oscar.

"NO!" wailed Herry.
"Well," said Oscar,
"I did find another doll.
  But it is not beautiful."
Herry stopped crying.
"Let me see it," he said.

Oscar hunted in his can.
Then he pulled out a doll.
"My doll!" yelled Herry happily.
"My beautiful, soft, fuzzy,
  sweet, cuddly doll!"
"Yucch!" said Oscar.

"Oh, Oscar!" said Herry.

"How can I ever thank you?"

"Just go away!" said Oscar.

Herry ran to Ernie and Bert's.
The party had started
and everyone was there.
So were their dolls.

Betty Lou had
a beautiful rag doll.

Grover had a soft,
fuzzy doll.

Cookie had a sweet
gingerbread man.

Big Bird had
a cuddly
bird doll.

And Herry had his beautiful, soft,
fuzzy, sweet, cuddly doll!
"I found my doll!" Herry shouted.
"Isn't he wonderful?"

Everyone was surprised.
Herry's doll did not look
like any of their dolls.
"Gee, Herry," said Ernie,
"your doll really IS wonderful.
He looks just like you!"